The Butterfly Effect

Part II

FaceOff

The Butterfly Effect

Part II

FaceOff

Channon Marie Watkins

Publisher's Note
Although inspired by actual events, this is a work of fiction. Names, characters, places, and situations are either used fictitiously or are products of the author's imagination.

ISBN: 9798365085527

Cover photo by Channon Marie Watkins

Published by WrightStufCo

www.wrightstuf.com
info@wrightstuf.com

Printed in the United States of America

SUMMARY

After learning of her heritage, Lisette left her grandmother's Bayou with newfound enlightenment. Now a junior at Xander University, located just minutes away from downtown New Orleans, Lisette encounters the ultimate faceoff with a mysterious component. Is it her new roommate, an age-old nemesis, or a new beau, or is she the dangerous force standing in her own way?

Faceoff (ˈfās ˌôf) a direct confrontation between two people or groups.

PROLOGUE

Twelve-year-old Lisette just entered her middle school locker room, with her teammates from the track team trailing beside her following her last victory of the season. Still gleaming with joy from her win, she set her trophy inside her locker as she changed from her track uniform back into her regular clothes.

Not really paying attention to those around her, she took off her track top and slipped her t-shirt over her head. She heard a couple of girls laugh, but when she looked in their direction, it was just the three of them looking at a phone.

She grabbed her trophy, closed her locker, and headed to the door.

"Congrats again, girl." Her friend Ariana said to her.

"Thanks," Lisette said as they high-fived each other.

The Next Day…

It was the last class of the day when Lisette received a message from Ariana.

Ariana: This was sent to me. Moriah took it yesterday, and she sent it to some boys on the football

team. I just wanted you to have a screenshot so you can report it because it's being sent around.

It was a photo of Lisette changing her top in the locker room after their last track meet. The caption read, "Trans or nah?" referring to her small breast size.

Lisette immediately sent the photo with its caption to her parents. She was humiliated.

Before that class ended, she was called to the principal's office. Both of her parents were there, and they were irate. Principal Moore assured them that the issue was being actively investigated and would not be taken lightly, but not before Lisette's parents let it be known that they were already "lawyered up" and ready to press charges.

As Lisette and her parents were walking out of the principal's office, Moriah and her parents were walking in, having just left a discussion with the assistant principal. Lisette stopped in her tracks. She couldn't move. She wanted to kill Moriah. Her feelings were hurt, but she was also incredibly angry. Lisette, very introverted, has never done nor said much of anything to Moriah. She didn't understand why this girl was targeting her.

"Lisette, do not say anything. Let's go." Her mother insisted, breaking her glare.

She looked at her mom and kept walking without saying a word.

Both Principal Moore and Moriah's parents scolded her. They scared her with words like probation, jail time, bullying, and child pornography. What she thought was just a joke had the potential to ruin her entire life.

That evening, Lisette, her siblings, and their parents discussed what had happened and made sure they knew not to discuss anything with anyone. After their talk, they all sat in the den as a family to watch a movie. About midway through, everyone's cell phone started getting notifications. At first, they thought it might have been a weather alert, but they all stopped when they realized Moriah had died.

"Oh my God!" Lisette screamed. "What happened?"

Shaken up, her mom said, "Give me a minute to find out..." She went outside to make a phone call.

"Lisette, come here. Listen, none of this has anything to do with you, ok? I don't know what happened to her, but regardless, you did nothing wrong." her dad said to her, assuming it had to have been a suicide.

Lisette nodded and just rested her head on his shoulder.

After a while, her mom came back inside.

"There was no evidence of foul play, no suicide note. Right now, it just looks like she died...She was at home with her parents. No one had visited..."

"That's crazy. How does a twelve year old just drop dead?" Lisette's dad asked.

Her mom only slightly raised an eyebrow, then she looked at Lisette.

"I think we should call it a night. It has been an incredibly long day. Go brush your teeth, say your prayers and go to bed...." Her mom said.

As the kids got up to leave, she continued, "Good night. I love you all."

"Good night," they said quietly.

That Summer...

"Mama, thank you for watching them today. Todd really couldn't get out of this business trip and I didn't want to leave them home all day. Not after what just happened. You know my kids are afraid of their own shadows." Lisette's mom said to her own mother.

"Oh, please. They are fine. You always acting like keeping my own grands is such a burden. I enjoy them." she said as she sipped her morning coffee.

"I know you do." Lisette's mom said with a smile.

"Did they ever find out what happened to that little girl?" Grandma asked.

"Her parents were being tight-lipped about it, but people are saying that her heart just stopped."

"Hmm..."

"Strange, right?"

"Indeed," Grandma said.

Lisette's mom stood up. "I have to go. They are calling for rain today, and the last thing I want is to get stuck on this Bayou. Thanks again, Mama." she said as she hugged her mother.

"Alright."

CHAPTER ONE

Beep! Beep! Beep! Lisette's morning alarm blared. She opened her eyes and stretched before she turned it off.

"Good morning," an unfamiliar voice spoke from inside the room.

Startled, Lisette jumped and almost tried to go through the wall her bed was positioned against.

It was the spring semester of her junior year at Xander University, and she had been without a roommate for five glorious weeks. The off-campus cottage had room for two upperclassmen and her previous roommate transferred to another school.

"Hi," Lisette said, after catching her breath.

"Sorry, I didn't mean to scare you." the new girl responded, holding a cardboard box. She was an average-sized girl who stood about 5'1". She had natural, tightly curled, dark brown hair.

"It's ok. Are you my new roommate?" Lisette asked.

"Yeah, my name is Blair. It's funny you didn't wake up the whole time I was moving my stuff in, but you popped up as soon as your alarm went off."

"Yeah, that is weird. I'm usually a light sleeper...I'm Lisette."

"And you sleep with your door open. That's weird too." Blair joked.

Lisette gave her a nervous smile. "It's nice to meet you. Are you new here...Or?"

"No, I'm a senior. My dorm room had plumbing issues, and I was next on the waiting list to move in here."

"Oh, ok."

"You have a class this morning?" Blair asked after she returned from placing the box in her bedroom.

"No, not until 1. I go for a run every morning. I'm on the track team."

"Oh, ok. Mind if I join you?"

"Not at all," Lisette said with a smile.

The girls went running through the wooded trail. There was a crisp chill in the air and a slight breeze. The girls' ponytails bounced as they steadily trudged uphill. It was a perfect morning. The sky was clear, the humidity was low, and it was just cool enough to see the fog from their breath. Running quick, but steady, the critters scattered at the sound of the girl's feet as they crushed the dried bark and twigs.

"Hey, are you ok if I speed up? I want to beat my last time." Lisette asked.

"Yeah, absolutely. I'm fine." Blair responded, nearly out of breath.

Lisette nodded and ran ahead of her while Blair maintained her pace. As Lisette picked up her speed, she caught up with some of her teammates and the coach's assistant, then passed them.

"Is this not in violation of some type of fraternization policy?" Lisette thought.

While Jolee was a member of the track team, she was also the coach's assistant, which made her an employee. Jolee has led the team through several undefeated seasons. The team was able to make room in their budget for a coach's assistant, so Jolee applied and was offered the position without hesitation.

Sisters Phoenix and Dakota were the other two girls running with her. They, along with Jolee, were the team's undefeated members of the girls' track team, and they felt like they were invincible. Some people refer to them as The Trinity. As Lisette ran past them, they sped up, and Jolee pushed Lisette, making her fall.

Blair saw the whole thing, so she sped up to help Lisette, but she was ok. The other girls didn't stop. They continued on the path.

"Are you ok?" Blair asked.

Lisette nodded as she stood up, "I'm fine."

"Why did they do that?" Blair asked.

"They only like each other. I'm used to it."

"That's not ok," Blair said.

"It's fine. Really. I've been in school with Jolee since middle school. She's never liked me." Lisette insisted.

Lisette and Blair went back to running together, trailing behind Jolee, Phoenix, and Dakota when all of a sudden, Jolee fell to the ground.

"Oh my God! Jolee, are you ok?!" they asked.

"My ankle! I don't know what happened. It hurts!" she whined.

"Man, karma's a bitch." Blair said as they ran past them.

CHAPTER TWO

"I don't think this is what the nurse meant when she said to keep my leg elevated," Jolee said.

The guy smirked, kissing her lips with her leg over his left shoulder. Wil Vaugh. Mr. Best All-Around. His mother is the first woman to be campus president, and she's currently in office. He's at the top of his class, and president of the Xander Honor Society, with his older brother and sister as his predecessors. His grades are remarkable, and he does volunteer work in his spare time. He's being groomed perfectly for a future in politics.

Wil and Jolee have been seeing each other for months, although no one knows. And for good reason.

She likes him, but Jolee doesn't want Wil to become a distraction. She is attending Xander on an athletic scholarship, and she doesn't want to let anything jeopardize that. Plus, she needs her job, and with her being considered an employee, their relationship could be prohibited despite them being classmates. She just wants to stay focused. She wasn't even sure if dating was something she wanted to do.

Before Jolee got ready to leave, Wil said, "Hey, there's a donor banquet coming up in a few weeks. You know my mom is expecting me to be there. You wanna come with me? I'm sure you can swindle some money for the athletic department."

Jolee smiled. "Donor parties aren't really my thing. I never ask for things. I just take them." she said as she smiled.

He smirked, "Are you going to the party in the SAC? I know you've heard about it."

"Yeah, that party is like two weeks away," she said with somewhat of an attitude.

A party was the farthest thing from her mind. She had a track meet in three days and she's not sure if her ankle will be well enough for her to compete.

"Yeah, but it's the first party of the semester. I was gonna drop in a little early before it got too rowdy. You going?" He asked.

She looked at him seated on his bed in just his boxers, then she looked away as she zipped her jacket.

"I'll let you know," she responded with a sigh.

Wil shook his head, and he looked away from her.

"What?" Jolee asked, picking up on his vibe.

"Nothing. You are just making it extremely clear what you want from me."

She rolled her eyes, "Wil, I like you. I just have a lot going on. You don't want these problems. You have no idea what it's like to be a student-athlete...Or, should I say, an injured student-athlete...with a job."

She walked closer to him and rested her arms on his shoulders. "I promise, you're the only one. I just can't fully commit myself to being in a relationship. It wouldn't be fair to you."

He took her arms from his shoulders, "I respect your honesty."

He knew, in that moment, he would not bring up the idea of doing anything further with her. He didn't even mention a relationship. All he did was ask to go to a party. Wil is a really nice guy, but he will never allow himself to be made a fool of. If she wanted to stay confined to his dorm room, then so be it.

After Jolee left, Wil went to shower. He shares a bathroom with one suitemate. A guy named Anton. This is their second year sharing a suite, and they have become pretty good friends over this time. They are a lot alike and share similar interests. However, while Wil is a political science major, Anton's major is physical education.

They both walked into their bathroom at the same time.

"Jolee?" Anton asked.

Wil sort of smirked, "Yeah."

Anton stepped out, letting Wil have the bathroom. Wil showered and changed into a pair of navy blue pants, a light pink polo, and a pair of brown shoes with a belt to match. He left his dorm and headed to the library with his bag draped over his right shoulder.

Wil got a table on the library's top floor where the reference materials were and put his bag down. As he searched for his book, he heard a thump. He thought he was alone, so he glanced around, but he was the only person on his aisle. Wil heard a few books crash to the floor on another aisle, so he went to see what was going on.

Lisette was there trying to get a book from the top shelf.

"Sorry if I disturbed you, I was trying to get one book, and three more came behind it," she said as she attempted to put one back.

"Not a problem."

He took it from her and placed it on the shelf. He bent down to get the other two, and he put them in place as well.

"Thank you," she said.

"Did you get the book you needed?"

"Yes," she said, showing it to him with a nervous smile. She was a little embarrassed, and she felt like a clutz.

"I don't think we've met. I'm Wil."

"I know who you are," she said.

"Wow, this is what happens when your family's reputation precedes you," he said with a smile.

She smiled and nodded, "Lisette," as she extended her hand.

He accepted it with a smile. "Well, it is nice to meet you."

"You as well."

Wil returned to the aisle he needed and Lisette took her book to her table.

CHAPTER THREE

"This wasn't your best meet, Jolee, but I don't want you to beat yourself up about it." Coach Ross said.

"Ok," Jolee said nonchalantly.

"I'm serious. I know it's bothering you, but you put entirely too much pressure on yourself."

Jolee was slouched in the chair across from Coach Ross's desk. The office was dimly lit and decorated with a few of Coach Ross's plaques and trophies that she had won over the years. Jolee was a tall, slender, dark brown-skinned girl with straight shoulder-length hair. She was wearing her emerald green track uniform and a jacket with the school's emblem on it.

A tear fell from her eye.

Coach Ross got up from behind her desk and closed her door.

"Jolee, you have one L. I don't think you've ever lost a meet before now. It's ok...You probably shouldn't have run today." she said.

"It still would've counted as a loss."

"Why are you so hard on yourself?"

"I just want to be great at something."

"You've been undefeated for three years. You have a full-ride scholarship, and your grades are still good...I'm sure your parents are proud of you."

"Parents? From which foster home?" she asked as she raised an eyebrow.

Coach Ross hesitated a moment before she responded.

"Oh, I didn't know."

"I never told you," Jolee said as she folded her arms.

Coach Ross sat back in her seat.

"I'm sorry," Jolee said, realizing how incredibly rude she was.

Plus, Coach Ross does not take attitude. She will retaliate with some type of physical punishment, whether it's planks or burpees, or now that Jolee works for her, she could make Jolee do practically anything.

"I went into foster care when I was eight years old, and I left the moment I turned eighteen. My high school guidance counselor was the only person I've ever told."

"That explains a lot of your aggression," Coach Ross said.

"You should've seen me before I started running track. One of the child psychiatrists I saw recommended it when I was about ten years old."

Coach Ross wasn't really sure how to respond.

"Jolee, everyone has a past. We all have things we'd like to forget. Some experiences being far worse than others. But you can't hold yourself to these virtually impossible standards. You are great, and I am proud of you."

Jolee eyed her strangely.

"No one has ever said that to me before."

"Have you ever been hugged?" Coach Ross asked.

"What kind of question is that?"

"A serious question."

Jolee crossed her legs and thought for a moment.

"My mom hugged me the last time I saw her."

"And when was that?"

"Maybe when I was five..."

Coach Ross stood up, "Come here."

Jolee stood, and Coach Ross embraced her.

"You have to let this anger go. You are only going to hurt yourself."

Jolee nodded and wiped a tear from her eye.

Coach Ross smiled, "Now, you better not tell any of your teammates I was nice to you. I will deny it. And if they see those tears, you let them think I chewed you out for losing today."

Jolee smiled, then sniffled, "Those bitches will never see me cry."

She wiped her eyes one last time and left Coach Ross's office. Coach Ross shook her head as she returned to her desk.

CHAPTER FOUR

Wil got to the party a little later than he had planned. It was already crowded from wall to wall. It was fairly dark except for the strobe light that was flickering. He walked in with Anton and began to make his rounds speaking to everyone. He didn't plan on staying long. Just long enough to get a few dances in and say he was there.

Lisette and Blair were also there.

"What's up!" Wil greeted Blair.

"Hey, how's it going?" Blair said.

"Not bad. Hey...Lisette?" Wil said.

She nodded with a smile.

"You two have met?" Blair asked.

"Yeah, we met in the library the other day," Lisette said.

"Oh, he won't give me credit, but I basically saved his life by tutoring him in Calculus," Blair said.

"I had the flu and got a week behind. That doesn't count." Wil said with a laugh.

Blair worked in the math lab as a tutor during her sophomore year. She and Wil are both seniors now.

"Sure...Well, you two talk." Blair said with a smile as she walked away.

No sooner than they started to speak, a friend of his excitedly pulled him away.

Lisette didn't think much of it. She walked away to find Blair, but no sooner than she spotted her, a guy came up behind her and started dancing. Lisette was fine with dancing with him, but he started groping her. She tried to nicely move his hands, but he was still persistent. She pushed his hands again and backed away from him.

"Quit acting like that," he said.

Blatantly intoxicated, he walked toward her. But, before she could even move, Wil stopped him. He placed his hand on the guy's chest.

"I think it's time for you to leave," Wil said.

"And who are you supposed to be?" the guy asked.

Wil stared coldly at the guy. That's when Lisette realized Wil's dark brown eyes were now red.

She quickly backed away and left the Student Activities Center.

"Lisette, wait!" Wil called.

The guy that had pushed up on Lisette now had a killer headache. He grabbed his head with both hands. Wil left him there and went after Lisette.

"Lisette!" he called.

She was already out the front door.

"Stay away from me," she said firmly, quickly walking toward the parking lot.

"Just listen."

"No, I know exactly what you are."

"What I am? I'm human. Lisette, we're just alike."

"How would you know?" she asked as she turned to him.

"Because I do. Tell me I'm lying..."

Lisette looked away, "I don't know."

"You've never used your power...."

She shook her head.

He looked at her for a moment. Her large curly fro was blowing in the night air. She crossed her arms, wearing a white off-the-shoulder shirt.

"At least let me walk you back to your car...I'm not gonna hurt you." Wil said.

"I know you aren't," she said softly, as she led the way.

Once they made it to the student parking lot, Lisette led the way to her car. She didn't get in right away; she eyed Wil. She could tell he wanted to say something.

"When did you find out about your power?" Wil asked.

"I'm not even sure if I have power. I've never hurt anyone or anything." Lisette responded.

"Yet."

"This isn't something I want...I've known about it since I was about twelve."

"Why don't you want it?"

"It doesn't represent anything good for me. It's like a curse on my family," she said.

"It's all in what you make of it...Who else in your family has it?"

"As far as I know, just my grandma and her sister."

"It usually skips a generation. I don't know how I got it because my mom does, but neither of my grandparents do."

Lisette got a text message from Blair.

Blair: Hey, where are you?

"I totally forgot about Blair," Lisette said aloud.

"Tell her to stay there, and we'll come back for her," Wil said.

Lisette: Stay there, Wil and I are headed that way. I left because this creep kept trying to feel me up.

After they picked up Blair, they went to the diner to hang out. When they got back on campus to take Wil to his dorm, he said, "Have a good night. Shoot me a text when y'all make it in."

They nodded before they left for the cottage.

...

Wil's dorm was practically empty because almost everyone was still at the party. When he got to his door, Jolee was standing there.

"I see you've made new friends," Jolee said.

He didn't respond. He unlocked his door and allowed her to walk in first.

"What's it to you?" he finally asked.

"Stay away from Lisette. I can't stand her," she said as she folded her arms and looked at him.

"Why?" he asked.

"Do I need a reason? Why can't you just do it?"

He noticed her shift her weight away from her right leg.

"Your ankle still hurts?" he asked.

"Yeah, and I didn't win my last meet. So you can imagine how frustrated I am."

"I bet."

"Yeah, so get naked."

He stared at her for a moment, then unbuttoned his shirt. She smiled as she crawled to the center of his bed.

CHAPTER FIVE

Jolee has been officially sidelined. Any running on her ankle could warrant permanent damage. She is out for the remainder of the season. Because of that, Dakota and Phoenix are no longer following her. She's no longer undefeated. But Lisette is.

Lisette walked into the gym with Dakota and Phoenix trailing beside her.

"You know, y'all can really do whatever workouts you want. Y'all don't have to do what I do. Everyone has their go-to." Lisette said.

"Your workouts are fine. The Trinity trains together." Phoenix said with a smile.

"Y'all actually go by that?" Lisette asked rhetorically.

As the three started their exercises, Lisette looked up and saw Wil running on the treadmill on the floor above them. She smiled, but more so with her eyes. He smiled back.

Jolee walked into the gym while they were working out.

"Wow. You two really have no loyalty. I thought you were my friends." she said to Phoenix and Dakota.

"We are your friends," Phoenix said.

"But you aren't one of us anymore," Dakota said.

"Seriously? I was the one who started The Trinity. I made y'all." Jolee said.

"You didn't win our races...And you didn't win your own, or else you'd still be one of us." Dakota said.

"Nice," she said sarcastically. "So, you think it's right for you to try and replace me...I hope you bitches remember this," she said.

Then, she gave Lisette this death stare. Lisette stood up from the exercise ball she was seated on.

After their workout, the girls went to the cafeteria.

"Ugh. Why is it so crowded?" Lisette asked.

"New Student Week. All of the new students are here for orientation. They moved the date up, so athletes can start training camp this summer." Phoenix said.

"Well, we see where our campus' priorities are," Lisette said.

"You're talking like you're not an athlete. Imagine if you were able to train with us all summer before your freshman year. You probably would've been better during cross-country. Then, Jolee might actually like you," Dakota said.

Lisette took a step back and eyed her, "I don't care if Jolee likes me or not. This isn't her track team. And if you're that concerned with her likes and dislikes, you can go join her," she said.

"Ok, let's just calm down. Both of y'all. Koti, that was out of line." Phoenix said.

Dakota only rolled her eyes.

Lisette got a text message. She looked at her phone, and it was a message from her brother.

Raphael: Turn around.

Lisette looked, and her brother was there.

"Raphie! Where have you been?! I haven't seen you all semester!" she asked excitedly as she dove into his arms. This is his senior year, and with him busy playing for Xander's baseball team and Lisette's running track, they haven't even been able to run into each other in months.

He tried to push her away by her face.

"Don't call me that out loud. Someone might hear you," Raphael said.

She laughed. "Why haven't I seen you? It's like we don't even go to the same school."

"I texted you months ago. You never respond to my messages,"

"Not true. Do you miss me?"

"Absolutely not. I just came to get food and saw you…For the first time in almost three months."

"Whatever," Lisette said dryly. "Well, I missed you." She hugged him.

"Cut it out. Why are you still annoying? You've been in college for three years now."

Lisette laughed as she took him to introduce him to her friends.

"This is my brother, Raphael. And this is Dakota and Phoenix." Lisette said.

"Nice to meet you. Are y'all twins?" he asked.

Dakota smiled. "No, she's older," she said as she pointed to her sister without taking her eyes off Raphael. "You look familiar…"

"You look like you play sports," Phoenix said as she stepped in front of her sister.

Raphael and Lisette exchanged glances. They were both a little embarrassed at how Phoenix and Dakota were throwing themselves at him.

"Yeah, uh, baseball," he said.

"You are on our baseball team. That's where I've seen you." Dakota said.

They both smiled at him.

"Yeah…Uh, well, I'll see y'all around. I have to go." he said.

"Bye, Lizzie!" he shouted to embarrass her.

She scowled at him, and he smiled as he walked away.

"Lizzie? Is that what your family calls you?" Dakota asked with a laugh.

"Yeah, Koti."

"I'd rather be Koti than Lizzie," Dakota said.

"Eh, maybe if I were a white boy," Lisette said as she turned away. "I'm not eating here. It's too crowded. I'm going to Tropical Smoothie.

Phoenix and Dakota followed behind her.

"Y'all are so childish. Nicknames aren't important right now. How old is your brother?" Phoenix asked.

"Twenty-two," Lisette responded with an eye roll.

"Ok...Do I really need to ask? I need specifics. What's his major? Is he single?" Phoenix continued.

"None of that matters because you're not dating my brother," Lisette said as she flashed a quick sarcastic smile before opening her car door.

When she got in the car, she texted her brother, hoping he hadn't left campus.

Lisette: Come have dinner with me!
Raphie: Are you still in the cafe?
Lisette: Just left. I'm in the car. I can come pick you up.
Raphie: I'll be in front of my dorm.

When Lisette and Raphie pulled up to Tropical Smoothie, Raphie immediately said, "I thought you said we were getting dinner?!"

"Bro, do better. They have food here. Healthy food. Like what athletes need." she said sarcastically.

After they got their food, they got themselves a table.

"I hear you're hot stuff now that Jolee is injured," Raphael said with a mouthful of food.

Lisette rolled her eyes, "You say it like she had to get injured in order for me to be hot."

"I don't mean you're not a good runner, but now you have your little band of followers...who have no subtlety, by the way."

"They actually call themselves The Trinity. I always thought it was a mean, not-so-inside joke...They take it seriously." Lisette replied before taking a bite of her wrap.

"That's not surprising." He said casually.

"And you know Jolee already couldn't stand me. Now she really freaking hates me."

"She has always seen you as a threat. You were her biggest competition until college." He took another big bite of his sandwich. "And if she wasn't older and didn't get a full year of training here before you, you'd probably still be better."

Lisette smiled, "That's encouraging, but no. Phoenix and Dakota are really good. They're both better than I am. I rank fourth on the team. Third, when you take Jolee out...."

He shrugged. "I guess. I heard their family donates like crazy money to the school. They probably pay off people to lose against them."

"You're funny," Lisette said. "We can't go this long without hanging out again. I get we'll both be home this summer, but we're at the same school."

"I have been insanely busy, but you're right," he said.

Later that evening...

There was a knock at Lisette's door. She paused her online lecture, snatched the earbud from her ear, then went to open the door.

She was a little surprised when Wil was standing there.

"Wil! Hey."

"Hi."

"Are you here for Blair? She's not home."

"No, I saw Blair a little earlier. She told me you'd be here. I'm here for you." he said.

"Oh?"

Wil smiled, "My mom is dragging me to a donor's banquet. It's Friday evening. Would you like to come with me?"

Lisette smiled, "Um…Yeah, sure. Why not?... What time should I be ready?"

Wil smiled, finding her nervousness slightly amusing. "I'll be here for you at 7."

"Ok," she responded with a nod.

"Uh, did you want to come in?" she asked, unsure of what to say next.

"I have a meeting to get to in about fifteen minutes...Raincheck?"

"Ok," she said as she nodded with a smile.

CHAPTER SIX

"Where are you going?" Dakota asked.

Track practice had just ended, and the girls were heading their separate ways.

"Why do you care?" Jolee responded.

Although Jolee couldn't run, she could still work out with the team, as long as she didn't do anything that would further injure her ankle, and fulfill her assistant duties.

"We're still your friends, Jolee," Phoenix responded.

"But am I still your friend?" Jolee asked rhetorically.

"Are you really acting like this because we're friends with Lisette?" Dakota asked.

"What do you mean? Am I acting like you two turned your backs on me the moment I got an injury? Mmh hmm." Jolee responded.

"Later," she said with a sarcastic grin as she turned to walk away. She almost walked into Coach Ross.

"Jolee, you need to report to student services by four o'clock." Coach Ross said.

"For what?" Jolee asked.

"I think this injury may be a bit much for you to take in. I think you need to see one of our counselors."

"Coach Ross, I'm fine."

"Let me make this clear for you. If you want to keep your job or stay a member of this team, you will report to student services every Thursday at four o'clock...Is that better?"

"Yes. Understood," Jolee responded, giving her the same sarcastic smile.

She waited until Coach walked away before she rolled her eyes. She made her way to student services and stormed inside, furious that she was being forced to see yet another counselor. It was like her childhood was happening all over again.

She signed in at the front desk. She looked at the guy standing behind the receptionists and rolled her eyes. He was one of her classmates interning in the office. She sighed, then went to sit back down.

"I swear this is a trap," she whispered.

CHAPTER SEVEN

Lisette was unsure of Wil's agenda. Does he really like her? Or is he just fascinated by the fact that she has power and refuses to use it? But she likes him, so she wants to go just to be with him and see exactly who he is.

On the night of the banquet, Lisette wore a black and white color block pencil skirt with an emerald green fitted long-sleeved shirt. She wore black pumps and pearl jewelry and pulled her thick, coarse curls up into a tight bun.

"You look so pretty. I wish y'all were going to something a little more fun than a donor banquet." Blair said, holding a make-up brush as she stood beside Lisette as they both looked in the mirror.

Lisette smiled. "I know, right. It'll be fine, though. I mean, how bad can it be?... Maybe I can talk someone into new track uniforms."

"Yeah."

There was a knock at the door.

Assuming it was Wil, Lisette went to open the door. A big smile came upon his face.

"You look beautiful," he said.

"Thank you," she responded.

"I won't wait up." Blair joked as the pair headed out.

...

"Mom, this is Lisette. She's a third-year, and she's undefeated on our track team." Wil said.

"Wow. Congratulations, and it's nice to meet you, Lisette." Dr. Vaughn said as they shook hands.

"Thanks. It's nice to meet you as well." Lisette said.

"How is your semester going academically?"

"It's going well. I'm still maintaining my grades."

"That's great to hear. If you ever need anything, don't hesitate to come to me."

"Thank you," Lisette responded with a smile.

"If you two will excuse me, the Hamiltons are on their second glass of champagne and should be in the giving spirit. I knew a cash bar was the way to go." Dr. Vaughn said.

She winked and walked away.

Lisette smirked, "She's nice."

"Most of the time," Wil said with a smirk.

When Lisette looked up, Raphael was walking toward them in a really nice suit she'd never seen him wear before.

She smiled, "Who are you, and what have you done with my brother?" she said.

He touched his collar, "I clean up well when I want to."

"He's your brother?" Wil asked as he and Raphael shook hands.

"He is," Lisette said. "How do y'all know each other."

"Um, I'm a part of the student council, Lizzie," Raphael said quietly.

Lisette smiled, feeling embarrassed. "I have been in my own little track world all semester, ok. Don't judge me."

Raphael only smiled, then someone caught his eye. "I'm gonna go speak to Dr. Prescott. Have fun," he said as he touched Lisette's arm and nodded at Wil before walking away.

As Lisette and Wil were standing there talking, she could sense the energy change in the room. They both looked in the same direction.

Jolee had just walked in. What was she doing there? Clearly, she wasn't invited. She wasn't even dressed for a formal event.

Jolee boldly approached Wil and Lisette. "Someone told me you were here with her, and I just had to see it with my own eyes," she said.

Lisette looked at Wil.

"Excuse me?" Wil said.

"I told you to stay away from her," Jolee said.

Dr. Vaughn quickly ended her conversation and went over to them. "Is everything ok?"

Jolee turned to Lisette, "You just couldn't stop until you had my life. I hope this feels great. You'll want to remember this feeling when it's all gone. And believe me. I'll make sure of it."

Dr. Vaughn eyed Jolee sternly.

Jolee conceded to Dr. Vaughn, "Yeah, I was just leaving,"

Dr. Vaughn stared at Wil with a look, telling him he better handle that situation. Wil quickly jumped in.

"Jolee, why don't we step outside to talk." He gestured for her to walk ahead of him.

Dr. Vaughn looked at Lisette, and she could tell Jolee's words had affected her.

"Come with me." Dr. Vaughn said.

Lisette followed her into the hallway. They stood in front of a large mirror. Dr. Vaughn lifted Lisette's chin and made her face the mirror.

"I want you to look in this mirror...You are a beautiful girl, and I can tell you're sweet as can be and incredibly smart. But obviously, you don't understand who you are."

She turned Lisette back to her.

"That girl came in here angry because you have everything she wants. You let her threaten you, and you actually felt threatened. That should never happen." She said as she pointed her finger.

"You never let anyone make you feel that way. You are not cursed. You are one of few women in this world who can control the respect she receives. And you need to demand it. From everyone...I don't want to see anyone be treated the way you just were, but especially you, because I know you can do something about it. You were born with power. Use it," she said sternly.

Lisette was a little afraid, but she nodded and looked back in the mirror at herself. Maybe Dr. Vaughn was right...

"Jolee, what is your problem?!" Wil demanded.

"I told you to stay away from her. Why couldn't you just do what I asked?" Jolee said.

"You can't tell me what to do or who to associate with. You didn't want me, remember."

"I thought you liked me," Jolee said.

"What does one thing have to do with the other?! You made it clear what you wanted. I told you I respected that. I'm not going to stop living my life. How is that fair?"

Jolee didn't respond.

"I think this has run its course. Let's just stop whatever we were doing before things go too far."

"What? You don't mean that," she said as she tried to put her hand against his face.

He grabbed her wrist before she could touch him. "I do. This is it," he said.

Jolee's mouth dropped. "Wow. First, it was my injury. Then, it was my friends. Now you're turning on me too...Wow," she said as her eyes welled up.

Wil looked like he was going to say something, but she held her hand up to stop him as she walked away. He went back inside just as Lisette and his mother were coming from the hallway. He walked over to where they were standing.

Dr. Vaughn chastised Wil, "I do not want to talk to you until tomorrow...If I were you, I'd make my way over to John Heathwood and try to talk him into some money for the law library."

Wil nodded and went to shake Mr. Heathwood's hand.

Dr. Vaughn turned towards Lisette, "You see the guy over there with the receding hairline and the goatee. That's Phoenix and Arizona's uncle."

"You mean Phoenix and Dakota?" Lisette corrected her.

"Whomever. If you want anything related to the track team or the athletic department in general, it's his wallet you want to get in. His name is Mr. Monroe. Introduce yourself, mention his nieces, and secure the bag," Dr. Vaughn said with a cordial smile.

Lisette nodded. After Dr. Vaughn went away, she finally exhaled and made her way over to Mr. Monroe.

By the time the party ended, Mr. Heathwood's company was writing a check for a very generous donation for the law library, and Mr. Monroe wrote a personal check for $50,000 to the athletic department. Mr. Monroe was the last to leave. Dr. Vaughn walked him out. "Thank you so much, Arty. It was a pleasure seeing you again."

"The pleasure was all mine."

Dr. Vaughn smiled. After he stepped outside, she closed the door behind him and rolled her eyes. "Finally, it's over," she said softly with an exhale.

Wil and Lisette were getting ready to leave. "Mom, do you want me to take you home?"

"No, I've already texted your father. He should be here any minute now. Y'all go ahead."

Wil nodded. Before they walked away, Dr. Vaughn touched his arm. "I like her," she said, referring to Lisette, then casually walked away.

Lisette smiled.

CHAPTER EIGHT

"Deputies are searching for twenty-one-year-old Xander University senior, Jolee Harris. It has been approximately thirty-six hours since she was last seen on campus…" the news reporter spoke candidly as Jolee's picture flashed across the television screen.

Blair turned off the TV.

"Jolee is missing?" Lisette said.

"That bitch is probably hiding somewhere. She's seeking attention." Blair said.

"I don't know. I hope she's ok." Lisette said.

"Do you think Jolee would be worried about you if you were the one that went missing?" Blair asked.

"What is with you?" Lisette asked.

"I just don't like her. The way she treats people is ridiculous."

"Yeah, but I'm sure she's like that because she has a larger issue. I still hope she's ok."

Blair just rolled her eyes as she stared into her phone.

The Next Morning…

Lisette got up for her morning run as usual.

"Are you coming?" She asked Blair.

"Are Thing 1 and Thing 2 gonna be there?" Blair asked, referring to Phoenix and Dakota.

"Probably. But it's ok. Come on."

Blair sighed, "You better be glad I'm still trying to lose this weight from my sophomore slump." She said.

"I've never heard of that," Lisette giggled.

"It's definitely a real thing…." Blair said as she stood up and stuck her foot into her shoe.

The two girls left and went to the trail. Phoenix and Dakota met them there, much to Blair's dismay.

They all kept the same pace as they were running steady and close, with Lisette and Phoenix slightly ahead.

"Oh my God!" Phoenix screamed, stopping dead in her tracks and causing Dakota to run into her.

Blair stopped. "What?!" she asked in a panic.

"It's Jolee." Lisette said.

The girls ran up to where she was lying along the trail.

"Jolee!" Dakota called.

"Jolee, can you hear us??" Phoenix asked.

Despite being missing for days, she looked like she was asleep. Her clothes were still clean, and she wasn't bleeding or anything.

"I'm gonna call 911," Blair said.

She and Lisette looked at each other. They were both thinking the same thing, but they didn't say anything.

Less than an hour later, there was police tape all around the area, and cops were everywhere. All classes were canceled for the week.

Jolee was dead.

A student died on campus, and no one had any idea what had happened. Students were scared. Parents were outraged. The entire campus was in an uproar. Wil and Dr. Vaughn came out to the scene.

"Are you all ok?" Dr. Vaughn asked as she touched Lisette's arm.

Lisette shrugged as her eyes welled up. Blair put her arm around her.

Wil and Dr. Vaughn stepped away. They went as close as they could without crossing the yellow tape. Jolee's body was covered with a white sheet.

"Damn," Wil said.

Dr. Vaughn exhaled, "I'll be back. I have to give a statement."

Wil nodded and returned to Lisette and Blair.

The following Friday, the school had a memorial for Jolee. Not only did they pay their respects to her, but the administration also tried their hardest to assure the students that campus safety was a top priority.

Coach Ross was giving remarks when Jolee walked in down the center aisle of the auditorium. Dr. Vaughn, standing beside Coach Ross for support, eyed her. She looked from Jolee to the other students.

No one reacted.

She looked at Wil, and his eyes were following Jolee. He gripped Blair's knee, and she put her hand on top of his, sharing his shock. Lisette was seated in the front row of the auditorium along with the rest of the track team. She gasped as she also saw Jolee.

Jolee walked onto the stage and sat so her legs could dangle over the edge. She flipped her hair across her shoulder and smiled deviously.

After the memorial, the four stood by the fountain in the center of the quad. The sound from the water was just loud enough to drown out their voices.

"Just to be clear, all four of us saw her inside that auditorium, right?" Dr. Vaughn asked.

They nodded.

"Blair, you have power?" Lisette asked.

Wil and Dr. Vaughn sighed.

"You still haven't told her?" Wil asked impatiently.

"I will," Blair said.

"What else is there for you to tell me?" Lisette asked.

"We'll talk when we get back to the house." She said. "Right now, we need to figure out why we're seeing Jolee."

"Did one of you kill her?" Dr. Vaughn asked blatantly.

They all looked at her as if they were offended.

"I'm being serious. There's no way for anyone to prove you did it if you used your power, but it will give us an explanation."

"Mom, did you do it?" Wil asked.

"Wil, that was someone's child. I'm a mother. I would never do that." She said.

"What? You stopped me from breathing for like a full minute when I was seventeen." Wil rebutted.

"I didn't kill you..." She said sternly.

He sighed, then looked away. "Well, if none of us did it, then who did?" He asked.

"Maybe that's what she wants us to figure out…." Dr. Vaughn said.

Blair sighed, "I guess it would've been too easy for this bitch to just die and go to heaven."

"Or not," Wil said as he raised an eyebrow.

"Try to have some respect for the dead." Dr. Vaughn said before turning to walk away.

"You two need to talk. I'll catch up with y'all later." Wil said.

CHAPTER NINE

The two girls headed towards the student parking lot.

"So, remember when I first moved into the house, and you slept the whole time…." Blair said cautiously.

"That was you…" Lisette said.

Blair nodded, and she stopped walking.

"Lisette, listen, I don't know any other way to tell you than to just come right out and say it...Analise and Sweetness are my grandparents…We're cousins."

"What?! That's impossible! And how do you know about them? If you think this is a joke, I'm not laughing." Lisette said.

"I don't think it's a joke. I'm not lying to you. I can take you to meet him...My grandfather."

"I don't understand...Sweetness left Analise on the bayou in a deep sleep." Lisette said.

"Who told you that?!"

"My grandmother…"

"Anmerie only knows what Analise told her," Blair said.

"Who says your story holds any more truth?" Lisette asked defensively.

"Me. I'm standing here looking you in your face telling you that my mother is Analise's daughter. Sweetness lives in the house I grew up in. He didn't leave her on that bayou until after my mom was born. They were married and everything. He loved her."

When the girls got to their house, they sat on Blair's bed. And as Blair started to talk, it was as if they were there. Standing in the yard as Sweetness approached Analise.

"Sweetness showed up at Analise's house the day after Quest was supposed to leave town.

'Hey, Hon.' he said as he approached the house. 'Hey! What you doing down in these parts?' she asked.

'I just wanted to come check on you.' he replied. 'Check on me? Why?'

'Well, you left out pretty fast Friday night.' 'Oh. Sweetness, I'm fine.'

He nodded, 'I see...You know that train pulled out yesterday evening. All the workers stopped by before they left.'

'Really? I bet that was delightful.' she said with a smile. 'Mmh hmm. All of the workers were there except for one." he said.

Analise turned to him, 'Oh?'

There was a long pause.

'Where is he?' Sweetness asked.

'How would I know?'

'He left with you.'

'Well, I'm not his keeper. I haven't seen him since Friday night.' Analise said casually.

Sweetness stepped onto the porch.

'Analise, I know what you've been doing. Did you kill that man?'

'I don't know what you're talking about. And who are you supposed to be? The police?'

'You know exactly what I'm talking about!' Sweetness scolded.

Analise started to get angry, and the vein in her forehead started to bulge. She didn't want to hurt Sweetness, but he might just have to be collateral damage. If, in fact, he does know Analise's secret, it could ruin her.

As she grew angrier, her eyes turned red, she waited for Sweetness's body to drop, but it didn't. He stepped toward her.

'That's not gonna work on me,' he said as he stepped closer to her. Afraid, she took a step back from him. 'Who are you?!' she asked.

'I'm still Sweetness...What? You think you're the only person in the world with a gift? You're in Louisiana. Almost every other person here is capable of something. You just lucked up and didn't run across them. Til now.'

'You get the hell away from me.' She said, as her voice trembled.

'Why? You've been doing this same thing for years. Haven't you? I could tell you had it from the first moment I saw you. But you're not as strong as I am. You saw nothing but a gentle spirit when you looked at me, didn't you?'

Analise nodded, and she stood against the front door. Sweetness smiled, 'That was intentional.'

Analise was afraid. Her intuition about Sweetness was all wrong, and now she felt like she couldn't trust herself. But she knew he was there to kill her.

'What do you want from me?'

'Tell me where that man is. There is a train full of people that saw him leave with you Friday night. It won't be long before they figure it out.'

'I didn't kill him. I left him in the hostel. If he's not still there, I don't know where he is.'

He eyed her suspiciously but knew she was telling the truth.

'You killed that man in my pub too, didn't you? The man that was standing in the corner.' he asked.

'He was gonna hurt me.' she said without looking directly at him.

'But, I was there! I wouldn't have let anything happen to you.'

'But I didn't know! Sweetness, I've been on my own for a long time now. I've never had anyone to look out for me.'

'You won't give anyone a chance! You won't let anyone near you. You kill every man that shows the slightest interest in you...That man hit the ground before I could even say anything to him.'

'I didn't know you were going to…' she said.

Still afraid of what he may do, a single tear fell from her eye as it started to change to its natural color.

Sweetness sighed, 'I'm not going to hurt you. I don't use my power for evil like you…I believe you when you say you didn't kill him.'

Analise nodded and wiped her face. Sweetness stood there for a few moments, then he turned to leave.

'Sweetness, wait…' Analise said.

He turned to face her.

'You say I won't give anyone a chance...Do you wanna come in?' she asked with a shrug.

This feeling of intense emotion and uncertainty was all new to Analise. She wasn't sure what she should do, but she knew she didn't want Sweetness out of her life.

Sweetness nodded and stepped onto the porch. She opened the door, and the two of them went inside.

Lisette was now feeling this same emotional uncertainty. How could Blair have lived with her all this time without telling her they were cousins? It wouldn't be such a big deal if their bloodline was not such a large part of who they are as individuals. But it shapes and molds their every thought and action.

She left the cottage and went to talk to Wil.

"Don't be so hard on her. She's been wanting to tell you for a long time." Wil said.

"Why are you taking up for her? What is with the two of you anyway?" Lisette asked out of anger.

"We're just friends. You know that," he said calmly.

"I don't know anything anymore!" she said while pacing the floor.

He quickly got up and ran into his bathroom. When he came back, he handed her a tissue, but not before the blood from her nose dripped on to her hand.

"How did you know that was going to happen?" she asked.

Wil nodded towards the mirror. She looked and noticed that her eyes were red.

She sighed as she flopped on his bed. Wil looked out his window as it began to rain.

"What about you and Jolee?" Lisette asked.

"What about us?"

"Why did she tell you to stay away from me?"

"Because she was jealous of you. But does it matter? Jolee isn't here anymore," he said.

Lisette shrugged and looked away.

Wil sat next to her. "What Jolee and I had doesn't matter anymore. I'm here with you, aren't I?"

She nodded.

There was a knock at Wil's door and Wil went over to answer it.

"Great, you both are here. I'm Detective Chase Dunbar. We need you to come down to the station.

Wil and Lisette looked at each other.

"For what?" Wil asked.

"Routine questioning. A twenty-one year old girl just turned up dead. Everyone on this campus is a person of interest. We're starting with the people who talked to her the night she disappeared."

Wil and Lisette looked at each other again.

"You can come with me now, or I can come back with a warrant. Then, I'll get to put you in handcuffs and escort you out," the detective said sarcastically.

Lisette got up and the two of them followed the cop out.

When they arrived at the police station, Detective Dunbar led them to a hallway where they needed to sit and wait to be called in for questioning.

Dr. Vaughn was already there.

"Mom, why are we here?" Wil asked softly.

"Jolee came to the donor banquet, remember. Apparently, she went missing not long after." Dr. Vaughn stated.

Lisette folded her arms, feeling uneasy about the whole situation.

"Remember, you don't have to answer anything that makes you uncomfortable without a lawyer present," she said.

They all nodded. A few minutes later, Anton entered the hall and sat across from Wil.

The three of them each looked sort of puzzled. Even Lisette could tell Anton didn't have power.

"What are you doing here?" Wil asked.

"Uh, I was asked to come in for questioning," Anton said nervously.

Wil could tell he was hiding something. He leaned forward toward Anton.

"Why? You saw Jolee the night she went missing?" Wil asked.

Anton looked away and scratched the back of his head, "Yeah...."

"Why?" Wil asked as his eyes began to turn red.

"Wil!" His mother said firmly as she placed her hand on his shoulder. "Save some questions for the police." Dr. Vaughn said nicely, trying to overshadow Wil's temper.

Dr. Vaughn stared at Anton until he drifted to sleep. The two of them looked at her.

"Listen," She said softly. "Do not let them get in your heads. Do not let them make you angry. Control your tempers."

She looked at Wil when she made that last statement.

"Only answer the question being asked, and do not confess to anything you didn't do." She continued.

Each of them nodded. A few moments later, Anton lifted his head. He looked around, trying to figure out what had happened. The three of them quickly looked away.

...

In the interview room....

Detective Dunbar leaned into Lisette's face.

"Were you friends with Jolee Harris?" he asked.

"No, we were teammates," Lisette said.

"I have, on good authority, reason to believe you two were enemies," he said.

Lisette didn't respond.

"Hello??" he said.

"You didn't ask me anything," Lisette said quietly.

"Were the two of you enemies?"

"I didn't consider her an enemy. Just a teammate."

"Was she just a teammate after you found out about her hitting a home run with your boyfriend?"

That comment surprised Lisette. Up until then, she could only speculate that Wil and Jolee had a thing.

"Oh, you didn't know?" Detective Dunbar asked rhetorically.

"I did not," she said.

"So when she confronted the two of you at the banquet, what did she say?" he asked.

"She said she had told him to stay away from me," Lisette said slowly.

"Exactly. And why do you think she wanted him to stay away from you? Because she didn't want him parking his ship in both ports!"

Lisette only rolled her eyes.

"So my guess is, maybe Jolee insulted you. It could've gotten physical...Maybe it was self-defense. Was it self-defense? We can work with that!"

"I never saw Jolee outside of the banquet hall. We've never gotten physical." Lisette said firmly.

"Oh...well, where did you go after the banquet?"

"Wil and I left together...and we went back to his dorm."

"Did you go back home that night?"

"I went back around six that morning," she said.

"Interesting...Did he take you back to the cottage?"

"No. He offered, but I told him I'd be fine with an Uber."

"Was your roommate in when you got there?" he asked.

"No."

"Really?... So here's what I think...You ran into her when you left Wil's dorm; she confronted you, things got physical."

"That's not true. I told you, inside the banquet hall was the last time I saw her." Lisette said.

"Oh, I heard you the first time you said it," he said. "Where was your roommate when you got in?"

"I don't know," I said.

"Ohh, so she fights your battles...Am I right?"

"No."

"Well, how can you be so sure?... Jolee's time of death was presumed to be Saturday morning around 6 a.m. You say you got up around that time and went home and your roommate wasn't there. How do we know she wasn't taking up for you? I know you told her about what happened. You probably "tweeted" about it the moment Jolee left," he said as he frowned his face up into a ball.

"Or maybe your boyfriend did it. Maybe he left his dorm not long after you and ran into her... Or maybe he even asked her to meet him...I'm sure he felt disrespected. I mean, he's Wil Vaughn. His mother's the president, for Christ's sake. He doesn't want a chick showing up to a formal event going all ghetto on him." Detective said.

Lisette only sighed.

...

"Wil Vaugh. Mr. Big Shot...Jolee was a liability. You didn't want her stirring up drama at a formal event. Your mom is the president. You're the big man on campus. You don't want it to look like you can't keep your women in check. So you got rid of the problem...Am I right?"

"No," Wil said.

"What did you do after Lisette left your room?" Detective Dunbar asked.

"I went to the freshman dorm next door because their snack machine has better choices. I got a Gatorade and a pack of Goldfish." Wil said with an arrogant smirk.

"Gatorade. Very funny. You really needed electrolytes?... And what time was this?"

"Around six."

"If I checked the security footage in the dorms, would that confirm your story?"

"Be my guest."

"I will. You know why? Because I don't believe you. I think you found out about Jolee and Anton and you snapped. She wasn't your girl, but you didn't want her with him either."

"I have no idea what you're talking about," Wil said.

"According to Anton, he and Jolee had been 'talking' for a while. He sealed the deal after you all kicked her out of that banquet. I think you already knew that."

"This is the first I'm hearing of it...I'm not even sure I believe it."

"Oh, it's true. His DNA was on her body. Why do you think he's even here?" Dunbar said sarcastically.

Wil didn't respond. He was quietly trying to control his temper like his mother told him.

"How does that make you feel? Are you angry?" Dunbar asked.

"No, I'm not angry. Jolee was free to see whomever she wanted...If Anton's DNA was on her body, why are you questioning me? Why am I being treated like a suspect?"

"Because you are a suspect." Detective Dunbar said coldly.

. . .

"Blair, where were you the night of the banquet?" Lisette asked curiously.

She hesitated for a moment, then she faced Lisette, who was standing in the doorway of her bedroom.

"I can't tell you. Believe me, Lisette, I want to, but I can't. I didn't kill Jolee, though. I didn't see her at all that day."

"Why can't you tell me where you were?"

"I just can't. Can you let it go and take me at my word?"

"I want to..."

"Just trust me on this..."

"Ok...But what is there to hide? You know you can trust me..."

"Plausible deniability," Blair mumbled.

"Huh?"

"I know I can trust you, but I'm protecting you by not telling you," Blair said.

Lisette didn't respond.

"I have to go," Blair said as she put her bag on her shoulder and left.

Lisette was still pondering about what Blair said. What could she possibly be hiding? She planned on questioning Blair further once she got back, but she stayed out all night.

The Next Day...

As Lisette was walking through the quad, she saw Blair walking at a brisk pace. She could tell she was on a mission. At this point, Lisette wasn't concerned about Jolee's death. This was pure curiosity.

She went in the direction that Blair was walking. As she kept a great distance between the two of them, Lisette couldn't help but wonder what in the world Blair was doing. She had followed her completely across campus to an area that was closed for renovation.

She watched Blair as she ascended the stairs to one of the buildings. She paused briefly in front of the door. Although the glass was dirty, she could still see her reflection. She ran her fingers over her hair and rubbed her lips together, making her gloss even, then she went inside.

After the door closed behind Blair, Lisette peeked through the dirty glass. She saw Blair walk into one of the old classrooms. She hesitated for a moment contemplating whether she should go in or not. Still, her curiosity got the best of her. She opened the door as quietly as possible and held it so it would close softly. She walked down the hall close to the wall.

"I was thinking we could get away this weekend. Just me and you. No hiding and sneaking around. I want us to see more than the inside of my house." A male voice said.

Lisette gasped and tried to get closer so she could peek inside.

"That would be refreshing," Blair said.

Lisette looked inside the classroom and saw Dr. Wallace, the head of the math department, seated on the desk, embracing Blair, who was standing in front of him. The two kissed just before Blair could sense the presence of someone else being there. She pulled away from him.

"Wait." She said as her eyes flashed red.

She went to the door and looked out into the hall, but no one was there. She sighed. In the back of her mind, she knew it was Lisette.

"What is it?" He asked.

"I thought I heard someone. I'm trippin'."

Dr. Wallace walked over and put his arms around her.

"So, is that a yes for this weekend?" He asked.

"Yes." She said as she smiled, then kissed his lips.

When Blair got back to the cottage, she confronted Lisette.

"Why did you follow me earlier?!"

"What are you talking about?" Lisette asked.

"Do not do that! You know exactly what I'm talking about. I know you were there. In the old STEM building...Why couldn't you have just left it alone?!"

Lisette sighed, feeling guilty. "Does he know I was there?" She asked.

"No, but that's not the point! This wasn't any of your business."

"I'm sorry."

"No, you aren't!"

"I am. I definitely overstepped."

"You did...Tell me, why are you going all 'Nancy Drew' for a bitch who didn't even like you? And to be honest, I haven't seen her since her memorial. I think you're the only one she's still haunting, so what does that say?" Blair asked as she folded her arms.

"I didn't kill her."

"How can we be so sure? You're so determined to pin her death on someone. Are you sure you aren't just trying to cover your own tracks?"

"I'm not! Me following you today had nothing to do with Jolee. I just wanted to know what you were hiding."

"Well, now you know. Do you feel better?" Blair asked sarcastically.

She stared at Lisette for a moment before she left her room. Lisette sighed, wishing she had minded her own business. Blair went to have dinner in the cafeteria on campus. Sitting there eating alone, she realized Lisette could really get her and Dr. Wallace in a lot of trouble.

"Ugh, I'm so stupid," Blair said softly.

Before finishing her meal, she got up, threw it away and headed back to the cottage.

Lisette was still there, sitting in front of her laptop.

"Here, I stole a Clif bar for you," Blair said as she tossed it on her bed.

"I'm not eating that!" Lisette said.

"It's unopened. I didn't do anything to it."

Lisette just looked at her.

"Why are you being nice to me?"

Blair sighed, "You could really get us in a lot of trouble..."

Lisette rolled her eyes.

"And," Blair said to keep her attention. "You're family. The two of us are probably more alike than any-one else in our family." She continued.

"You're right...And I am sorry for getting into your business. Besides, plausible deniability still stands. You didn't see me follow you. You never told me anything."

"Oh no, you lost your protection for yourself," Blair said as she sat beside Lisette, making herself comfortable. "Keith and I have been seeing each other for a while now. About eight months, actually."

"Keith?"

"That's Dr. Wallace's first name," Blair nodded.

"I don't want to know anything else," Lisette said.

"I'm not really sure how it all happened. It feels like it happened so fast—

"You don't have to tell me any more," Lisette interrupted.

"No, you implicated yourself. So now, if he and I get in trouble, so will you. For not telling."

"Then, I'll go ahead and tell," Lisette said, trying to stand her ground.

Blair folded her arms and glared at Lisette with red eyes, "You sure you wanna do that?"

Lisette wasn't afraid, but knew she was fighting a pointless battle because she would never purposely get Blair in trouble.

"How do you know how he really feels about you?" Lisette asked.

"My power tells me..."

"That's it?"

"I would love to say that I got this feeling that he's just different. Like my inner self just knew. But that's not the case. Every guy I've dated had what I considered an 'it' factor. It didn't always work out. Once I used my power, I was able to tell right away. Maybe my regular "women's intuition" is broken, but I prefer this anyway."

"Can I ask you something? And I feel completely awkward for even having to bring this up," Lisette asked.

"What is it?"

"How are you able to contain your power when you have sex?... I mean, both my grandma and Analise almost killed their lovers at first."

Blair looked at her for a moment, then smirked, "The same way everyone else does, I guess. What's your method?"

Lisette looked away. "I don't have a method."

Blair sort of wrinkled her brow. "Wait, what? Am I understanding you correctly?"

Lisette nodded.

"You're a virgin?"

Lisette nodded again.

"Aww!" Blair said sympathetically.

"Ok. Can we please not do this? I've never had a really serious relationship, so I've never felt comfortable enough to sleep with anyone...But now I do, and I'm terrified."

"Why? Lisette, you're not gonna kill him." Blair said with somewhat of a smirk. "He has power too. He's actually very strong. You'll be fine…For me, I had already gained control of my power before I lost my virginity. It was still difficult. I was in my head a lot, but it gets easier...But you won't have to worry about that. Wil can take care of himself."

Lisette nodded. "Thanks."

"Wait. So, the night of the banquet, when you said you got back at six in the morning…"

Lisette shook her head, letting Blair know that nothing sexual happened between her and Wil that night.

"Well, what were you doing?"

Lisette smirked, "Talking."

"Sheesh," Blair said as she covered her face.

"Does Dr. Wallace have power?" Lisette asked.

"Keith. And no, he doesn't, but his dad does, so that means our hypothetical kid is likely to have it since it skipped him…."

"So he knows about your power?"

"Yeah. He caught me using it one day. I never kill anyone. That's the one thing my grandfather drilled into me. But I do make it possible for certain things to happen. Kind of like The Butterfly Effect. Like how Jolee accidentally stepped on a twig and sprained her ankle."

"That was you!?"

"What, you thought that was actually karma?" Blair asked with a smirk.

"Wow."

"I was in the math lab just about to start a tutoring session when this guy told me that he didn't want me to tutor him. He wanted 'the Urkel-looking, brainiac.' Because there was no way I could help him in Accelerated Calculus I, even though I took it two years ago. So I set him up with an appointment with Oliver, and as he was leaving, he casually walked into a display and a huge book fell on his crotch."

Lisette laughed.

"Not only did Keith hear what happened, he also saw it because his office door was open, and he called me out about it…I tried to play it off, but then I realized not only did he already know, he liked it. After that, the chemistry between us was undeniable."

"Aww. That's almost like a fairy tale for people like us." Lisette mused.

"No, you're living the fairy tale and don't even realize it," Blair said.

"You think so?"

"Absolutely. Wil's a good guy. I mean, he let himself get played by Jolee. But the fact that you've waited twenty-one years and now you're having these feelings isn't coincidental...I'm not telling you what to do, I'm just saying, don't be afraid if you think it is what you want to do. If you're worried about him, don't be."

Lisette smiled and nodded, "Thanks."

...

About a month after that conversation with Blair, Lisette found herself lying in Wil's bed with her blouse tossed on the floor and her pants unbuttoned. Wil held her by the nape of her neck and he pulled her in and kissed her. Without a second thought, she put her arms around him and pulled him closer. She paused when Wil put his hand on the waistband of her pants.

"Wait. I have to tell you something." Lisette said.

He moved his hand from her waist.

"I've never done this before."

"Ok. It's ok. We don't have to."

"No. I want to. I just thought you should know."

"Are you sure?"

Lisette nodded, then kissed him. She tried her best to do as Blair said and try not to be "in her head." However, she could tell when her power began to take over. She held the sides of Wil's face and kissed him long and hard. Wil let out a sound, but she purposely didn't let that distract her. She dug her nails into his back as her eyes turned blood red.

Wil rolled over, glistening in sweat, and laid flat on his back.

"*Oh, God. Is he ok*?" Lisette thought to herself as she glanced over at him, holding the sheet over her body.

"Are you ok?" Wil asked.

Lisette smiled and nodded. Wil extended his arm and Lisette laid her head on his chest. Hearing his heartbeat was the most satisfying sound. She smiled to herself, perfectly content with her decision. She closed her eyes briefly, listening to him begin to snore lightly. When she opened her eyes, Jolee was leaning against the window in the room, looking at the two of them. However, she was gone before Lisette could even react.

The next morning, Wil sat up and touched where Lisette scratched his back. It was still tender and beginning to itch from where it was starting to scab.

Lisette asked Wil, "Were you in love with Jolee?" She was still lying in bed. Lisette had her back to him, and his arm was wrapped around her waist.

"Absolutely not. Why would you ask that?"

She rolled over to face him and she shrugged her shoulders.

He sighed, "Jolee and I were just…friends with benefits." He said slowly.

"Is that what we are?"

"Lisette, don't be crazy. You've met my mother...Is that what you think of us?"

"No, but I don't really know what to think anymore."

"Clearly, you're overthinking. Stop it...We're together."

Lisette smiled.

"What is with this rival you had with Jolee anyway? She didn't want me near you. Now, you're bringing her up...What is it?"

Lisette looked away and then got out of bed.

"I don't know." She said as she stepped into her pants.

"Why don't I believe you?"

She sighed as she looked at him. She put her shirt over her head then pulled her hair from her collar.

Wil moved to the foot of the bed.

"Obviously, you two weren't best friends. I gathered that."

CHAPTER TEN

Summer

Lisette stepped inside Grandma's house for the first time all year. She purposely stayed away from her grandmother now that she has been more in-tune with her power. She knew her grandmother would pick up on it and didn't want her to know.

When she walked inside, Grandma surfaced from the back with a blanket she was crocheting.

"Hey, baby," she said as she hugged her.

"Hey, grandma. I've missed you."

"Aw. You could've fooled me. Where have you been hiding?"

Lisette nervously smiled. Why did she think she could outsmart her grandmother?

"I wasn't hiding...There was just a lot going on."

"Mmh hmm."

They stepped into the kitchen.

"Come look at this new coffee maker your mama got me. It's so fancy." Grandma said proudly.

Lisette walked over to the counter. "It's a Keurig," she said casually.

"And it doesn't leave coffee grinds behind," grandma said happily. "Would you like a cup?" she asked.

"Sure," Lisette said with a smirk. She sat at the kitchen nook, then grandma came over carrying two cups of coffee. She sat in front of her.

"So, you gonna tell me what you got yourself into?"

Lisette sighed and shrugged. "Have you ever felt like history was repeating itself?"

"All the time. But, what do you mean?" Grandma asked.

"Remember that summer when we got stranded here and you told us about Analise?"

Grandma nodded.

"Well, ever since then, I think I've had the same powers you were telling us about."

"I know you did. Why do you think I told you the story?"

Lisette didn't respond.

"I've been trying to ignore it, and I haven't used it at all, but the past few months have been crazy." She covered her face, "...And now this girl is dead...And I think it's my fault," she continued as she started to cry.

"What did you do?" Grandma asked.

"I don't know. I never tried to hurt her, but she still haunts me."

"Why?" Grandma asked sternly.

"It was no secret that she hated me. She made my life miserable every single day. The night she went missing, she came to me and said some really mean things, but I never retaliated. Two days later, we found her dead, and now her spirit is still haunting us...."

"Who is this 'us' you speak of?"

"My roommate Blair, our friend Wil, and his mom, our campus president. We all have power, and we all saw her."

Grandma put her hand against Lisette's cheek. Lisette felt as if she were comforting her, but she didn't know that by doing this, Grandma could see small bits of what had happened.

As she looked into Lisette's eyes, she could see the girls running on the trail. She could see the party in the SAC, she saw the fountain in the quad, and the donor banquet, then suddenly, she saw a snake as it leaped toward her. She jumped and quickly snatched her hand away.

"Grandma, what's wrong?"

"There is an enemy in your circle. I can't tell who it is, but one of them can't be trusted. You walk around with this guilt when it has nothing to do with you. And that's exactly what they want."

"Are you sure? I don't know who it can be."

"You have to be careful. Sometimes it's the person you trust the most."

"Wait, are you saying they killed her?"

"I can't say yes or no. Does any of them have a motive to want her dead?"

"I don't know, but this just made things a lot more complicated. One person is blood, and the other I thought I loved...And they both looked me in my face and told me they didn't do it."

"You have to be careful. You need to rely on your power and your instinct now more than ever."

Lisette sighed, nodded, then took a long, pensive sip from her coffee cup.

CHAPTER ELEVEN

Lisette walked into her brother's room while he was playing his video game.

"What's up?" He said without taking his eyes from the screen.

"Hey. I wanna talk to you about something."

He paused the game and looked at her. "Are you ok?" he asked.

She nodded and sat beside him.

"Is this about Jolee?"

"No. Well, sort of...do you remember when grandma told us that crazy ghost story?"

"You mean when she told us she was a vampire?" he asked as he stood up.

"Grandma is not a vampire."

"Lizzie, you were there! Her eyes were red!" He said.

Lisette just looked at him.

"I mean, I think having a vampire grandma is pretty dope." He said with a shrug.

"Anyway, this isn't the purpose of the conversation. I wanted to know if you felt any differently since hearing that story." Lisette inquired without saying too much.

"Different how? Like how I feel about grandma?"

"No..." She paused for a moment. She wanted to know if he had the power, but she didn't want to outwardly ask. She also didn't want him to know she had it because he may not understand it. A new theory came to mind.

Anmerie didn't get the power until after she slept with Quest. Lisette didn't gain control of her power until she'd been with Wil.

"You've had sex, haven't you?" she blurted out.

Raphael looked at her as if she had a second head.

"What?! We are not having this conversation." He said.

He picked up his gym bag and placed the strap over his shoulder.

"If mom asks, I'm going to the park to play ball," he said as he walked away.

Lisette sighed as he left the room.

...

Lisette felt literally drained. She was sitting on her bed, and she started to cry.

"Dry your face. I don't do tears." Analise said.

Lisette wasn't the least bit startled. She lifted her head and looked directly into Analise's eyes. She wiped her eyes with her hand.

"I don't know what to do…." Lisette said.

"Well, crying in your room isn't going to help you. Trust me, I would know...I spent a year and a half in a deep depression over that damn Sweetness," she said as she sat on Lisette's bed.

"What happened? I know the two of you had a daughter…."

Analise sighed as she crossed her legs.

"I might as well tell you since everyone else wants to tell my story," she said. "Sweetness and I were great together, but he is such a nice and gentle soul, and I'm not...The difference between you and me is that I don't give people a chance to hurt me. Jolee would've been dead the first day I met her...That's one thing Sweetness didn't like about me. He didn't want our daughter growing up thinking that was ok. And neither did I, but it was my natural instinct. It got to the point where Sweetness decided he was taking our daughter and leaving.

As much as I hated him and myself, deep down, I understood him and knew it was for the best. I didn't understand why my mom gave Anmerie away until that happened. I understood, but it didn't hurt any less. I was in depression from the day Sweetness left 'til the day Anmerie and Quest showed up on my porch... Now, what's your problem?"

"Somehow, I have managed to practically sever every relationship I've built over this girl who didn't even like me. Why am I still seeing her? I mean, why me?! Is this just her fulfilling her promise to keep me away from Wil? Because it's working."

"I don't think I've ever encountered anyone who's hated their powers more than me," Analise said as she eyed Lisette strangely.

"Listen, I don't know why Jolee chose you, but there is a reason. You have been so preoccupied that you still have not taken the time to even acknowledge all of the power you have. You are way more gifted than I was. You have vision. Do you realize, the entire time your grandmother told you my story, you saw the whole thing as if it were happening right in front of you?"

"I guess I did…I didn't think about that," she said.

"Take some time to yourself. Get away. Go for a walk or run. You need to find yourself first. Then, you'll realize your answers are right in front of you."

Lisette smiled, and that's when she realized Analise came to her. She stared at her for a moment, admiring her brown curls and how they both looked the exact same age, even though Analise died decades ago. She saw so many features that reminded her of her grandmother and even more that reminded her of Blair.

"Thank you." she finally said.

Unsure of what to say next, Lisette looked down for just a moment, and when she looked back up, Analise was gone, just that fast. Without so much as a second thought, Lisette changed into her running clothes. She grabbed her earbuds, but then she thought for a moment and put them back on her bed. She left her room, not exactly sure where she was headed.

"Where are you going this time of night?" her mom asked.

"I just need to go out and clear my mind...I'll be fine. I'll be back in a little while," she said.

Her mom hesitated at first, but she reluctantly nodded.

Lisette got in her car and drove to Xander's campus. She parked in the student lot, got out, and started walking in the direction of the track trail. When she got there, she got to her usual starting point, set her timer, and started running. With no music, all she heard was the ground beneath her feet and her heart rate increasing. She finished the lap thirty-six seconds faster than her last run.

She stood at her starting point, breathing heavily and she went again. As she ran, she began to feel more tired than usual and slowed down.

"How is this gift of vision supposed to help me? So what if I can see what people are telling me? Unless someone is gonna tell me what happened to Jolee, I won't be any help." Lisette thought.

She kept walking as her pace continued to slow down. She exhaled as her heart rate returned to its normal rhythm. She wiped the sweat from her forehead back across her hair as she continued on the path, lost in the sound of her footsteps against the ground of the wooded trail. The rhythm changed when she stepped on something. She pulled the item from the bottom of her shoe. It was a Xander University baseball pin.

All of a sudden, something changed. She wasn't alone anymore. Her defenses quickly went up. With now red eyes, she turned to see who was behind her.

It was Jolee. But it wasn't Jolee's ghost. It was Jolee from the night of the banquet. She wore an emerald green tracksuit with a white tank and white sneakers. She sniffled as she walked by slowly.

Lisette was confused as Jolee walked past her as if she wasn't even there.

"This is that night," Lisette said quietly.

She followed Jolee through the trail, walking slowly behind her. A tall, dark figure briskly approached them.

"Oh no, it was Wil." she thought, feeling a terrible knot in her stomach.

She stopped walking, and her heart started racing.

"No," she whined softly as her eyes stung with tears.

As he got closer, she realized,

"Wait. That isn't Wil," she said aloud.

She quickly walked toward the pair. The guy was wearing a black Xander University hoodie with the hood pulled over his head.

Jolee stopped walking as the guy was standing directly in her path.

He took his hood off.

"Do I know you?" Jolee asked.

"Raphael! No!" Lisette yelled.

But it was useless. They couldn't hear her. She was merely watching a not-so-instant replay of that night.

Before Lisette could even get the words out, Jolee's body had hit the ground, and Raphael rushed past her. The pin fell from the pocket of his hoodie.

As Lisette came back to reality, she looked at the pin in the palm of her hand and she struggled to even let out a sound. She fell to her knees. Her tears stung her eyes, and she could no longer stand.

"No. No, Raphie. How could you?" she said.

She covered her face for a moment and when she looked up, Jolee was there.

"You're welcome," Jolee said.

Lisette stood up, "Excuse me?"

"Let's not pretend like this is gonna be some sentimental moment. We helped each other out. Now, you know your boyfriend isn't a murderer, although your brother is...And I can finally cross over," she exhaled. "So, you're welcome."

It took Lisette a moment because she was taken aback by that comment.

"Well, you're welcome," Lisette said.

Jolee smirked, "Bye, loser." She said as she pushed past Lisette.

Lisette turned around and Jolee was gone.

"There is no way she just went to heaven...Not even possible," she said.

Despite Lisette's conflicted feelings about Jolee's death, she finally felt a sense of peace. She was livid that her brother could do such a thing. Not only did he pretend like nothing had happened, but he acted like he had no idea such power existed. On the other hand, she was so relieved that Wil didn't do it and she could have her life back.

When she got back home, Lisette stormed into Raphael's room. Her eyes were red, and she wanted to kill him for lying to her.

"You liar!" she yelled. "Get up!" she said as she snatched him from his bed.

She surprised herself with the amount of strength she realized she had.

"What is wrong with you?!" Raphael asked.

"Not only did you lie, but you also tried to make me think I was crazy! You acted like you didn't even know these powers existed," she said, still holding the collar of his shirt.

He snatched her hand away, but she could tell by the amount of force that he used that he was using his powers and he wanted her to know it.

"Lizzie, stop it. I don't know what you're talking about," he said firmly.

"I know you killed Jolee!" she shouted.

With red eyes, Raphael grabbed Lisette by the shoulders and pushed her away. "I said I don't know what you're talking about. Now, let it go!" he yelled firmly.

"I'm not afraid of you! What are you gonna do? Are you gonna kill me too?" she asked as she pushed him with both hands.

Because of her strength, he slammed into the wall. The ruckus caused their mom to come and see what was going on. All she saw was Raphael charging toward Lisette. He lifted her up by her neck, but she kneed him in his stomach.

"What in the world is going on? Stop it!" Mom yelled, "Put her down!"

They completely ignored her. When Lisette kneed Raphael, he barely flinched. She used almost all of her strength and punched him in the face. He dropped her, and then they began to tussle. He pushed her away with so much force she put a small crack into the wall.

"Oh my God!" she said as she ran between them.

She looked from her son to her daughter, both panting with red eyes.

"Stop it. Please. I need you both to calm down," she said with her arms stretched out, trying to keep them away from each other.

"Mom, move," Lisette said calmly.

Raphael didn't say anything. He just stared at Lisette.

Their mom sighed, "Analise, if you can hear me or see this, now would be a really good time to show up," Mom said softly.

No sooner than their mom whispered those words, she fell to the floor, and Analise appeared. Raphael and Lisette looked from their mom to Analise.

"She's fine," Analise said nonchalantly.

Then she looked at the two of them. "What is your problem? You two are just gonna fight until one of you dies?" Then she looked directly at Raphael, "You gonna kill your sister?"

"No," he said quickly.

"Then cut it out. You're tearing up this room for no reason." Then she turned to Lisette. "Let this go. I told you what you needed to do for you to get peace of mind. It's over. You have to accept that you're just not like your brother. He's a protector. He will always be that way, just like me. He has his reasons. Deal with it. Or not...But do not summon me over this again," she said.

Lisette nodded.

Analise disappeared within the blink of an eye, and Mom sat up from the floor. Raphael went to help her up, but she pushed him away. She stood up.

"Analise came?" she asked.

They both nodded without saying anything.

"How long has this been going on?" she asked.

They both shrugged.

Lisette started, "I've had the powers for a long time, but I just started using them this year."

"I started in high school," Raphael mumbled.

"Does Delia or Marcel have power?" she asked as if she were exhausted.

"Mom, we didn't even know each other had power until just now," Lisette said.

Mom sighed and walked away, but before she left the room, she said, "Do not ever fight in my house like that again."

"I started it. We're sorry," Lisette said softly.

"It won't happen again," Raphael said.

Without responding, their mom closed the door and went back to bed.

Lisette and Raphael looked at each other. Solemnly, Lisette exhaled and leaned against the wall and Raphael sat on his bed.

Lisette slid down to the floor. "Why did you do it?" she asked as tears began to fill her eyes.

"Jolee wasn't a good person. She knew you killed her friend in middle school, and she wanted to hurt you. She needed to be stopped."

"I didn't kill anyone. What are you talking about?"

"Moriah. You think she really had a heart attack at twelve years old?"

"But I was at home when she died. We were all here."

"Lizzie, you were twelve. You weren't nearly as strong as you are now. Mom told grandma that you saw Moriah in the office after y'all talked to the principal, she stopped you from saying anything, but then she died that night...Just think about it."

Tears started to fall down Lisette's face. "Then, conveniently, Grandma told us the story...She told me she knew I had it and that's why she told the story to begin with...."

"Exactly," Raphael said quietly.

"How do you know all of this about Jolee? Are you sure she knew?"

"Your coach made her go to counseling after her injury. I'm a psych major, obviously, so I had to complete 200 clinical hours. I had full access to all the files, so I read hers...She had been through a lot, so not all of her sessions were about you. When she did mention you, she said you took her place on the track team just like you took away her best friend. She said she hated you and couldn't wait for you to get what was coming. According to her chart, she had a plan...I wasn't going to sit back and wait to see what her plan was. I didn't care about Jolee or her feelings. I didn't care about what she went through in her past. I don't have compassion. What I cared about was the fact that she had a plan for my sister. It didn't matter what the plan was. I stopped it."

Lisette sighed. "I don't know what to say…Do I thank you for killing someone?"

"Does it really matter if she's dead or alive? Is your life not better with her gone?" he asked.

Lisette hesitated, "Raphie, don't make me answer that."

"Lizzie, just let it all go. No one can prove I killed her. I don't have to worry about you, and now you can go live your life. Go try to be normal."

About the Author

Channon Marie Watkins is a native of Columbia, South Carolina. She earned a bachelor's degree in English Literary Studies from Columbia College in South Carolina, where she attributes her writing and analytical skills.

Raised as an only child, Ms. Watkins was always encouraged to use her imagination during playtime. As time passed, she became an avid reader, and writing soon followed.

The Butterfly Effect Part II is her second published book. Check out The Butterfly Effect, Parts I and II on Amazon.com and other online bookstores. There's more to come. Be on the lookout.

www.ingramcontent.com/pod-product-compliance
Lightning Source LLC
LaVergne TN
LVHW091029150826
845672LV00006BA/1751

9798365085527